T0169064

Worzel says hello!

Will you be my friend?

Written by Catherine Pickles
Illustrated by Chantal Bourgonje

Hubble & Hattie

I hope you like my Mum's book. She wrote it so that children and dogs can have a great time together throughout their lives. This is the first book in a series that will show you everything dogs and children can do together, happily and safely.

Love from
Worzel Wooface

PS If you know any grownups who like dogs, tell them about the books I wrote!

The Hubble & Hattie imprint was launched in 2009 and is named in memory of two very special Westie sisters owned by Veloce's proprietors. Since the first book, many more have been added to the list, all with the same underlying objective: to be of real benefit to the species they cover, at the same time promoting compassion, understanding and respect between all animals (including human ones!) All Hubble & Hattie publications offer ethical, high quality content and presentation, plus great value for money.

www.hubbleandhattie.com

First published September 2017 by Veloce Publishing Limited, Veloce House, Parkway Farm Business Park, Middle Farm Way, Poundbury, Dorchester, Dorset, DT1 3AR, England. Fax 01305 250479/email info@hubbleandhattie.com/web www.hubbleandhattie.com. ISBN: 978-1-787111-60-8 UPC: 6-36847-01160-4
Readers with ideas for books about animals, or animal-related topics, are invited to write to the editorial director of Veloce Publishing at the above address. British Library Cataloguing in Publication Data – A catalogue record for this book is available from the British Library. Typesetting, design and page make-up all by Veloce Publishing Ltd on Apple Mac. Printed in India by Replika Press.

Foreword

Knowledge is a great ingredient, but it's not the complete recipe.

If we're to educate our children, and enable them to receive the kind of love we (you!) know only a dog can give, there are other essential ingredients we need to throw into the mix: empathy, perspective, patience, and kindness.

Combined with the rock solid wisdom threaded throughout *Worzel says hello!* these essential ingredients blend together to produce a beautiful and important book for all to enjoy.

The text is underpinned with sound canine knowledge, and delivered in an easy-to-understand, easy-to-apply manner that not only gifts the reader with an enjoyable read, but also equips him or her with the vital tools required to live a life loving, cherishing, and respecting our four-legged friends.

Oh, and the illustrations (I know you've had a sneaky peak!). Gorgeous.

I'm a fan!

Steve Mann
Chairman
Institute of Modern Dog Trainers (IMDT)

Introduction

For as long as I've written about Worzel, I have yearned to create a book about him for children. As a parent, a teacher, and, of course, a dog lover, I was determined to do this in a way that would have a positive impact. Whilst I have written three adult books about Worzel, it is *this* book that makes me the most proud.

When I was young, my brother and I were taught by our Mum how to safely interact with dogs. Our respect for dogs meant they would choose to come for a cuddle with us on the sofa, and trust us when we played with them. When we met new dogs out and about, we knew to wait until the owner invited us to say hello to their dog, and we stood still and waited for the dog to come to us, rather than excitedly rushing up to them.

These are the lessons I passed on to my children, and they are skills that every child should know.

Whether you are a dog owner, a teacher, a parent, or simply want your child to be better equipped to feel the love and companionship of doggy friends, it's my hope that this book will enable children to have safe and positive relationships with dogs. Equally, I hope this book will help adults to have more confidence in their ability to support the children and dogs in their care.

Catherine

All interactions between children and dogs should be supervised by an adult.

Parental Advice

Children and dogs can be the best of friends, and good for each other in so many ways. Many adults will fondly remember a childhood dog who helped them through a hard time simply by being there as a constant companion they could confide in without being judged, or curl up with when they needed comfort.

Sadly, though, dogs are often misunderstood by both adults and children, and their behaviour can be misread. It is important to remember that dogs and children should always be supervised when together, so that everyone stays happy and safe.

In this book, Catherine and her Lurcher, Worzel, take you on a journey, where you will gain an understanding of how dogs think and feel, so that all children can have a wonderful relationship with the dogs in their lives, and all dogs can feel happy, safe, and loved.

Rachel Hayball ISCP Dip Canine Prac, VSPDT
Animal Behaviour & Training Council (ABTC)
Registered Accredited Animal Behaviourist

I really want to say hello

I really, really do

But I am Worzel Wooface

And I'm scared of you

I wasn't treated gently

when I was very small

And even now I'm all grown up, I'm not that brave at all

When you meet me, please stand still

And I will come to you

Let me sniff you
once or twice

It's not that
hard to do

Don't try to stroke
me straight away

Don't wave

your hands about

Let me check you're kind and safe

Don't squeal
or yell
or shout

Let me walk around you

Please pretend that I'm not there

You can stroke
me when I'm sure

You won't give
me a scare

Watch my
tail begin
to wag

A little dance I'll do

And if you feel me lick or nudge

I'd like a stroke from you

Now I'm happy!

Now we're friends!

Now I'll take a treat

Please do it all again like this
The next time that we meet

I'm really glad we said hello
I hope you think so, too

I am Worzel Wooface

And I'm not scared of you

Catherine and Worzel

Catherine Pickles is a teacher, parent, full time family carer, and Worzel's mum. She has owned dogs all her life, and regularly fosters for Hounds First Sighthound Rescue. Author of three hilarious adult books about Worzel, this is her first children's book about him. She lives in Suffolk with her husband, Mike, two children, five cats, and of course, Worzel.

Worzel

Initially a foster dog, from the second Worzel skidded through the door, Catherine knew that he would be her first 'failed foster' – and Worzel Wooface was adopted permanently from Hounds First Sighthound Rescue.

Worzel's early puppy experiences were dreadful and he is easily frightened. Despite this, he loves to meet children and adults alike. Over the years, Catherine has developed a way of introducing him to people that is positive for all concerned. This story follows those rules, and provides a great guide for children about how to greet new dogs, regardless of their background.

Worzel blogs and writes a regular column for his local newspaper. He is a champion for rescue dogs, and considers himself a Rescue Ambassador, promoting the joys and challenges of second-hand dogs.

In 2016, Worzel won a Heroes of Dog Fest award.

Chantal

Chantal Bourgonje is a Dutch illustrator and writer of picture books, working from her home in the Wiltshire countryside, where she lives with her partner and two Whippets.

Chantal's inspiration comes from nature, the countryside, and the living creatures in it.

In 2011, Chantal graduated with a 1:1 Honours degree in Illustration.

Her graduation project was highly commended in the MacMillan Prize, and, in 2013, she was highly commended in the AOI Awards. Since graduating, Chantal has written and illustrated children's picture books, one of which was awarded a Kirkus Star for books of remarkable merit.